Follow Anna's adventures in these books:

The Year of the Book

A JUNIOR LIBRARY GUILD SELECTION
"A pleasure to read and more. This is a novel
to treasure and share with every middle-grade
reader you know."
—*New York Times Book Review*

The Year of the Baby

A JUNIOR LIBRARY GUILD SELECTION
★ "This book deals deftly with a range
of thorny adoption—and ethnic—
stereotyping issues."
—*School Library Journal*, starred review

The Year of the Fortune Cookie

A JUNIOR LIBRARY GUILD SELECTION
"A pitch-perfect sequel."
—*School Library Journal*

The Year of the Three Sisters

"This unique sisterhood beats with a gentle
heart." —*Kirkus Reviews*

"Cheng's characters are as charming as ever.
Another winner." —*School Library Journal*

The Year of the Garden

* AN ANNA WANG NOVEL *

by Andrea Cheng

illustrations by Patrice Barton

Houghton Mifflin Harcourt
Boston New York

The text of this book is set in ITC Berkeley Oldstyle.

The Library of Congress has cataloged the hardcover edition as follows:
Names: Cheng, Andrea, author. | Barton, Patrice, 1955– illustrator.
Title: The year of the garden / Andrea Cheng with illustrations by Patrice Barton.
Description: Boston ; New York : Houghton Mifflin Harcourt, [2017] | Series: An
Anna Wang novel ; 5 | Summary: "Follows perceptive, astute Anna as she strives
to grow a perfect garden—only to realize that the garden she grows with her
new friend is more than good enough, weeds and all." —Provided by publisher.
Identifiers: LCCN 2016001791
Subjects: LCSH: Chinese Americans—Juvenile fiction. | CYAC: Chinese
Americans—Fiction. | Friendship—Fiction. | Gardening—Fiction. | Moving,
Household—Fiction.
Classification: LCC PZ7.C41943 Yi 2017 | DDC [Fic]—dc23
LC record available at https://lccn.loc.gov/2016001791

ISBN: 978-0-544-66444-9 hardcover
ISBN: 978-1-328-90017-3 paperback

Printed in the United States
DOC 10 9 8 7 6 5 4 3 2 1
4500704988

To Lena
—A.C.

To Natalie and Jeorgia
—P.B.

Laura

Me, Anna Wang

CONTENTS

PRONUNCIATION GUIDE

Happy New Year - *Xin nian kuai le*

(*shin nien kwai le*) 新年快乐

Red Envelope - *Hong bao* (*hong bow*) 红包

Dumpling - *bao zi* (*bow dse*) 包子

Thank you - *xie xie* (*shieh shieh*) 谢谢

You're welcome - *bu xie* (*boo shieh*) 不谢

Chapter One
Seeds

Every Saturday morning, Mom cleans the Shepherds' house. My brother, Ken, and I usually go with her.

"How do you like your new home?" Mrs. Shepherd asks as soon as Mom opens the door.

"Very good," Mom says, taking her bucket to the kitchen sink and turning on the water. "So much space for kids."

"Let me know if there's anything you need. We have lots of things stored in the basement." Mrs. Shepherd turns to my brother and me. "Just yesterday I was cleaning out the closet, and I set aside a few things for you."

We follow Mrs. Shepherd into the bedroom, and I notice that one of her legs is dragging. She holds on to the doorframe to keep her balance, then sits down in the armchair. Next to it is a cardboard box with a big envelope on top. "Whenever you get mail, it has a mark from the place it originated. Mr. Shepherd and I feel like we traveled the world with this postmark collection."

"Don't you want to keep it?" Ken asks.

"There comes a time when a person gets tired of traveling." Mrs. Shepherd hands Ken the envelope, then looks up at me. "And, Anna, here are some of the books and magazines I read when I was a girl. I figured, what good are they gathering dust on a shelf?" Mrs. Shepherd stops for a minute to catch her breath. "This one was my favorite." She hands me a thick book with a red cover called *The Secret Garden.* "I think this book is the reason I turned into a gardener." Mrs. Shepherd leans back in her chair. "And it's probably the reason I turned into a reader, too. Now you kids make yourself at home while I rest a bit."

Ken and I spend the afternoon matching the postmarks to a map of the United States that was folded up in the envelope. Then Mr. Shepherd sets out a bowl of pretzels and a pitcher of lemonade.

"Come join us for a snack, Mary," he says. But Mom isn't done dusting the living room. "Your mother is a real treasure," Mr. Shepherd says. "And you kids, too."

Ken stacks a bunch of pretzels on his finger and eats them one at a time, dropping crumbs all over the table. I glare at him, but he keeps on nibbling.

"Never mind." Mr. Shepherd sweeps the crumbs into his hand and rolls his wheelchair over to the door so he can throw them into the backyard. "Better than bird seed." He points to a tree. "See that? A yellow finch just waiting for a snack."

When Mom says it's time to go, Mrs. Shepherd comes out of the bedroom holding a small paper bag. "I have one more thing for you, Anna. I harvested the seeds from our garden, and I thought maybe in your new house you'd have someplace to plant them."

"Don't you want to plant them here?" I ask. "In your garden?"

Mrs. Shepherd looks out the back window. "You know, Anna, my gardening days are over." I follow her gaze to the flowerbed. Most of the plants are brown and dry, but there are still some orange blossoms around the border. "The seeds are labeled so you'll know what's what."

"Thank you," I say. Ever since I can remember, I wished I lived on a farm with a big vegetable garden and a barn full of hay where Ken and I could play hide-and-seek and jump from one bale of hay to another.

We head down the street to the bus stop. The wind feels hot and humid, as if it might rain. When we get to the orange bus stop sign, I turn back. Mr. Shepherd has wheeled himself out to the front porch. Mrs. Shepherd is standing beside him, leaning on his chair. I wave and they wave back. When the bus comes, they are still waving.

Now that we moved into our new house, the bus ride home takes longer. I wish we were going back to our old apartment at Manor Court. Then when we got home, I would go next door to see if Suzanne could come out. At our new house, I don't know anyone and I don't have anything to do.

I put my hand into my pocket and feel the paper

bag with the seeds inside. Maybe I really can find a place at our new house for a garden, like behind the back porch. Since our house is on the corner, we do have lots of space. Dad said he wouldn't have time to tackle the yard until next year, but I can clear the land myself, just like Pa and Ma in *Little House in the Big Woods*. I can cut down the bushes and dig out the roots. Ken can help me take out the rocks. Then, in the spring, I can plant Mrs. Shepherd's seeds.

Chapter Two

Laura

On Sunday after lunch, Dad heads to work. He's trying to pick up extra shifts to pay for repairs to our house. He wants to redo the wiring first, and then we need to buy paint for the walls.

After she washes the dishes, Mom sits at the small card table to study her English vocabulary words. She writes each word on the front of a file card, and on the back she writes the meaning in Chinese characters. She goes through the stack of cards, closing her eyes to remember. Sometimes she asks me how to pronounce the words, like *affordable* and *economy*. But no matter how many times she repeats the words, they never sound exactly right.

I look outside. The house across the street has the curtains drawn against the sun. Nobody is out. I get *The Secret Garden,* open the door, and step outside.

One of the honeysuckle bushes in our side yard has overhanging branches that form a cool space underneath. I crawl inside and sit down on a flat stone that seems to be waiting for me. I run my hand over the cover of the book. The material used to be rough, but now it is worn smooth and the corners of the cover are rounded. The book even smells old. I try to imagine Mrs. Shepherd when she was my age, opening this same book cover, but I cannot picture her face without deep wrinkles around her grayish eyes.

I turn to the first page. Mary Lennox lives in India and she has servants who take care of her. She orders them around as if she is in charge. She is spoiled and selfish, but it's not her fault. Nobody really pays much attention to her, and she is alone most of the time. Even though

she's not very nice, I feel sorry for Mary and I want to keep reading.

Suddenly a girl about my age crawls into the space underneath the bush. "I was walking my dog up to the corner, and I thought I saw someone back here. My name's Laura."

It takes me a second to realize that I am not in my book world with Mary. "My name's Anna."

"I'm eight," Laura says.

"Me too."

"When's your birthday?"

"March nineteenth."

Laura smiles. "Mine's March twentieth. What school are you going to?"

"We just moved in . . . I think the school's called Pleasant Hill."

"Me too!" Laura sits down right next to me on the flat rock. "I can't believe that we have almost the same birthday and we both just moved in. And my middle name is Ann, which is close to Anna. What's your middle name?"

I have to think fast because my middle name is Chinese and I can't pronounce it. "I don't have one."

"What are you reading?" Laura asks.

I show her the cover.

"That book looks antique." She scratches a mosquito bite on her ankle. "My mom and I really like old stuff."

"Where did you used to live?" I ask.

"Indiana," she says. "With my aunt. It's country there."

"Really? With a farmhouse and a barn?"

Laura nods. "They have a horse, three dogs, four cats, and lots of chickens." She makes a little mound of dirt with her fingers. "I love animals." She looks up. "Do you have any pets?"

I shake my head. "My mom says I'm not old enough to take care of them."

Laura pulls her eyebrows together. "We've had pets since before I was born. Our first dog died, but now we have a German shepherd named Lily and a cat named Liliana. Where'd you live before?"

"Here in Cincinnati. At Manor Court."

"What's that?"

"An apartment complex."

Laura wrinkles her nose. "Was it a slum?"

"What's that?" I ask.

"I mean, really poor?"

"No," I say quickly. "Just a regular apartment."

Laura stands, reaches for the branch above her, and hangs for a minute. "This honeysuckle is as big as a tree," she says, wrapping her legs around the branch and pulling herself up. I grab the same branch, hook my legs around, and hang upside down. Something falls out of my pocket and lands on the dirt.

"What's that?" Laura asks.

"Seeds," I say, I flipping around and jumping to the ground at the same time as Laura.

She picks up the bag and reads *marigolds, mixed lettuce, chocolate cherry tomatoes, green beans, pickling cucumbers.* "I don't really like vegetables," Laura says. "But chocolate cherry tomatoes sound good."

"Do you think they really taste like chocolate?"

"I don't know," I say.

Laura pushes her hair away from her face. "We could plant the seeds at my aunt's farm. She has a really big garden."

Mrs. Shepherd thought we might have space for a garden at my new house. I don't want to take her seeds so far away. And if the garden is in Indiana, I won't be able to work on it as soon as I wake up every morning. "We could make a garden here," I say.

Laura looks around. "I think a garden has to be flat and it can't have bushes everywhere."

I point toward the middle of the backyard. "That part is pretty flat. We could dig out the weeds and then turn over the soil. You know, like pioneers."

Laura stands up so fast, she hits her head on the

honeysuckle branch. "First we have to decide exactly where," she says, rubbing the top of her head.

All afternoon we work. We decide to use the bigger stones to mark the border of our garden. Some of them are really heavy so we carry them together. When we run out of stones, we find more in the gully behind our house.

Laura holds a worm in her hand. "Earthworms are good for a garden," she says, setting it gently on the soil. "Plus, they attract birds, and I love birds. Woodpeckers are my favorite. What about you?"

"I don't know much about birds," I say.

We drag the stones into place, matching the ends like the pieces of a puzzle. The only breaks we take are to get drinks and go to the bathroom. By the time Mom calls me for dinner, we have three sides of the border done. I don't think I've ever had so much fun in my whole life.

Laura wipes her hands on her jeans. "I never made a garden before."

"Me either."

"It's harder than I thought." She looks at the stones we've put into place. "My aunt's garden has all these sections, for flowers and lettuce and corn." Laura scratches her stomach. "And each section has a little fence around it. I think it'd be easier just to use her garden."

"I want to plant the seeds here," I say. My voice sounds louder than I expected.

Laura looks away. "In Indiana, it's really country—you know, with big fields and cows."

"There's lots of space here," I say. "We just need to pull out the weeds and dig up the bushes."

Laura shrugs, then heads up to the sidewalk. She turns back. "My house is on the other side of the street, about halfway down. The one with a cat painted on the mailbox."

She runs down the hill with her blond hair flying.

Chapter Three

Pleasant Hill School

As soon as I wake up, I remember that today is our appointment at Pleasant Hill School. We have to make sure everything is in order before the first day. My stomach feels tight. In less than a week, I will be a third-grader.

It's not even nine o'clock, but already the sun is hot. Mom and Ken and I walk down the hill. "That's Laura's house," I say, spotting the cat painted on the mailbox.

Mom isn't listening. She wants us to hurry even though our appointment isn't until nine thirty. Ken's light blue button-down shirt is dark where the sweat soaked in. Mom wanted me to wear a summer dress, but I insisted on wearing my new jeans, which are scratchy, and a red long-sleeved shirt. We turn down Pleasant Street. The school is at the end of the block.

When we open the door of the building, the cold air rushes out. *At least Pleasant Hill has air conditioning,* I think, following Mom into the main office. Sutton School had only fans, which blew our papers around. Once it got so hot that Mrs. Mallory let us eat popsicles in our classroom.

The secretary asks us to sign in.

"I am Mrs. Wang," Mom says, trying to pronounce our last name the way Americans do so it rhymes with *bang* instead of the way it's supposed to sound, which rhymes with *song.*

The secretary looks us up on the computer. "You must be Anna," she says to me. "And this is Ken. Welcome to Pleasant Hill." She gives us two envelopes that have our names on the outside. Then she asks us to wait until the vice principal comes to give us a tour of the school.

Mrs. Kyle is very tall with a heap of blond hair on top of her head. "Good morning," she says, holding her hand out to Mom.

Mom shakes her hand. "Nice to meet you."

"Let's start with the library," Mrs. Kyle says. Her high-heeled shoes make a loud clicking sound in the hallway. This school is much bigger than our old school, and everything is new. "I'm guessing you like to read." She looks at me and I wonder how she knows.

Mom nods. "Yes, Anna reads big books."

I wish she wouldn't say that.

The library is bright and has beanbag chairs in

back. I want to lie down in one and keep reading *The Secret Garden* instead of following Mrs. Kyle all over the building.

Finally she takes us to our classrooms. Ken will be downstairs with the first- and second-graders in room 107. Mrs. Kyle opens the room with a key and we peek inside. There are round tables with small chairs and a climbing structure in back.

"Do you want to go in?" Mrs. Kyle asks Ken.

He shakes his head and I can tell from his eyes that he's scared.

Next we head upstairs to the third and fourth grade classrooms, and Mrs. Kyle opens 207. "This is Mr. Ellis's room," she says. "He will be your new teacher."

The desks are arranged in groups of four. There are posters on the wall with pictures of plants and animals, and an empty aquarium on the back shelf. "What's in there?" Ken asks in a voice so soft we can hardly hear.

"Last year they had a turtle," Mrs. Kyle says. "I'm not sure what Mr. Ellis has in mind this year."

Mr. Ellis. I say the name in my head a few times, trying to imagine who Mr. Ellis could be. I never had a teacher who was a man before. If I were still at Sutton, I would know where everything was. I could say hi to Mrs. Mallory on the first day of school. She would have a book waiting for me. And I would be in a class with Suzanne.

After the tour, Mrs. Kyle asks us if we have any questions. I want to ask if Laura will be in my class, but I don't even know her last name.

"Thank you for show us the school," Mom says. *Showing,* I want to whisper.

❋ ❋ ❋

"I wish we were still going to Sutton," I say on the way home.

Mom puts her hand on my shoulder.

"I think Sutton was a good school," I say.

"Pleasant Hill is good too," Mom says. "Give a chance."

I run ahead of my mom and my brother. When I get to Laura's house, I think of knocking on the door to see if she wants to come over and work on the garden, but my jeans are too hot and I don't know her parents or her brothers. There is a big dog sleeping in the front yard. That must be Lily, but I don't know if she's friendly to strangers. I hurry past the house.

When I get home, I change into shorts, grab my book, and go outside to read under the honeysuckle bush. When Mary is exploring around her new home in England, she finds a very old rusty key. Then, in the next chapter, she is jumping rope when a gust of wind blows the ivy, and behind it is a doorknob with a keyhole. The old key fits into the lock, and Mary slips into the secret garden.

I stop reading and look up at the overhanging branches. For a minute, I think I am in the world of ivy and climbing roses and stone walls covered with moss. On the first page of the chapter, there is a picture of Mary Lennox opening the garden door. She looks just like Laura.

Chapter Four

Clearing the Land

In the morning, Laura rings our doorbell. "Want to play?" she asks.

"Let's start clearing the land," I say, putting on my shoes.

Laura looks doubtful for a minute, then follows me to the backyard. "Just like pioneers," I say, breaking a honeysuckle branch.

"My great-great-grandparents really were pioneers," Laura says. "They went from England to Massachusetts on a big ship, and then they came to Ohio in a covered wagon."

"Really?" I never knew anyone who was related to a real pioneer.

Laura nods. "My grandma told me."

"I bet they cleared the land just like this." I toss a branch outside the border of the garden.

"What about your great-great-grandparents?" Laura asks.

"I don't know."

Laura looks up. "Did they come from Japan?"

"China," I say, feeling my cheeks flush. Suddenly I wish I didn't have an Asian face and that my ancestors were pioneers too. My one grandma lives in China where Mom was born, and my other grandma lives in California.

"Cool," Laura says. "Have you ever been to China?"

"Once," I say. "But I was little so I hardly remember."

"Can you talk Chinese?"

I shake my head. "Not much. My dad doesn't speak it, and my mom's trying to learn English."

Laura looks interested. She says she wants to go to

lots of places like Asia and Africa. "The farthest away I've ever been is Michigan. And that's only eight hours by car."

"I've never been to Michigan," I say.

We work for a while without talking—breaking branches, pulling out weeds, and digging out rocks. Clearing the land is hard, but I don't mind getting sweaty and I love the feeling of making something so real. After we finish pulling out the weeds, we can decide where to plant everything. We can mark different sections for tomatoes, lettuce, and beans. The marigolds will look pretty around the edges. We can even make a gate out of wood like the one in the secret garden, with ivy hanging all around. And next fall, we will have chocolate cherry tomatoes to share with the Shepherds.

"I hope we'll be in the same class," Laura says. I am thinking so hard about the garden that I almost forgot about Laura.

"Me too. Maybe they'll put the new kids together." I pull out a big thistle weed, careful not to touch the thorns. "I think if I was a principal, I'd do that."

I've found a way to get the honeysuckles out by the roots. I put the blade of the shovel near the base, jump on the top edge with both feet, and then push the handle down. The whole root ball pops out of the ground, flinging dirt all over the place.

Laura struggles with a thick branch. She twists it around but it still won't snap. Finally she lets go and it dangles like a broken arm. "Want to take a break?"

It seems as if we just started. "Already?"

Laura's cheeks are red and her face is sweaty. She wipes her forehead with the bottom of her T-shirt. "Want to get a drink?"

If we take breaks all the time, how will we ever finish the garden? In *Little House in the Big Woods* they worked all day without stopping until sunset. I almost tell Laura to go get a drink out of the hose, but I know that wouldn't be very nice. Then I see someone walking up the street with a plate in her hands.

"Welcome to the neighborhood," Laura's mom

shouts. "I hear the two of you have quite a project going back there." She heads to our front door. "I brought these for your family."

"My mom makes the best cookies," Laura says, wiping her hands on her jeans. "Let's go have some."

I follow Laura to our back door.

Laura and her mom have the same blue eyes and they both talk in fast spurts. "Just wanted to say hello and introduce myself," Laura's mom says to Mom. "My name's Diane, Diane Morgan."

"I am Mary," Mom says. "Mary Wang."

"We're so happy that Laura and Anna are the same age," Mrs. Morgan says.

Mom nods. "Yes, a friend is very nice."

"I have to run errands, but I did want to tell you that we have a neighborhood walking group Wednesday mornings and a book club Thursday evenings."

"Thank you," Mom says. "I really appreciate." But I don't think Mom will have time to take walks in the morning because she has houses to clean, and she can't read that well in English.

"Okay, I have to run," Mrs. Morgan says, setting the cookies down on the card table. "Enjoy."

"Thank you," Mom says again.

Mrs. Morgan turns back. "Let us know if you need anything." She smiles. "We just moved in a few weeks before you did. So we're both new to the neighborhood."

After Mrs. Morgan leaves, Mom goes back to her flash cards. I take out two glasses, set them on the counter, and fill them with milk. Laura takes a cookie and dips it in.

"I love chocolate chip cookies," she says, taking a big bite of the soggy cookie. "What kind is your favorite?"

"Chocolate chip too," I say, even though my favorite snack is bean paste buns.

Laura smiles. "Figures. It's almost like we're twins." She takes a big gulp of milk. "We're going to Michigan

ANDREA CHENG

tomorrow. We have a cabin there. And we're not coming back until right before school starts."

"A log cabin?"

"Sort of. It's on a lake."

I finish my milk. "Ready?"

I can tell Laura doesn't want to go back out to work
on the garden. "Do you want to play cards first?" she
asks.

"I don't think we have a full deck," I say, even though
I know there's one in Ken's desk drawer.

"We have lots of decks," Laura says. "I can run and
get one."

"Let's keep working," I say, pushing the screen door
open.

Laura follows me out into the backyard jungle.

Chapter Five

Last Day of Summer

$\mathcal{T}$he phone rings. "We can come now," Mom says. She turns to Dad. "That was Mr. Shepherd. Mrs. Shepherd is not feeling well."

Mom, Dad, Ken, and I get into the car and head over.

Mrs. Shepherd is lying on the sofa in the living room with her eyes closed.

"Elsa was sorting through her things, and next thing I know, she's all slumped over," Mr. Shepherd says.

Dad thinks we should call an ambulance to take Mrs. Shepherd to the hospital, but when she hears that, she shakes her head.

"We can take you to check," Mom says.

"No," she whispers.

"You know Elsa—she's a stubborn one," Mr. Shepherd says. "The more you try to convince her of something, the less likely she'll do it." He refolds the washcloth against her head. "She's been that way all her life, at least the past sixty-six years that I've known her. And I don't suppose she'll change anytime soon."

"Maybe that is good," Mom says, going into the kitchen to heat up some water.

Mom gets Mrs. Shepherd to sit up and have a cup of tea with a few crackers. Dad goes to the grocery store to pick up soda and a bag of ice. Ken and I sit at the table and make get-well cards. I draw a big orange marigold on the front of mine.

"We started our garden," I tell Mrs. Shepherd.

She sets down her teacup and her face lights up. "So you did find a spot. Clearing the land—that's the hard part." She looks at Mr. Shepherd. "You remember, Sylvan?"

"Do I ever," he says.

"If you get it cleared out now, you'll be ready come spring." Mrs. Shepherd's voice gets stronger as she talks. "Plant the lettuce first. It's not much for heat, you know." I give her the marigold get-well card and she pulls me close. "You know what's special about these flowers?" she says. "They keep the bugs away."

When Dad gets back, Mrs. Shepherd has a few sips of ginger ale. Then Mom and I help her to bed. We make sure the covers are just right and I bring a glass of water to the night table. Mr. Shepherd brings the get-well cards and sets them next to the glass. Mrs. Shepherd closes her eyes and we tiptoe out of the room.

It's past ten, but I still can't sleep. With the sheet, I feel too hot, but without it, I'm shivering. I turn on my light and open *The Secret Garden*. Mary has just discovered a sickly boy named Colin. When the two of them are together, Mary forgets that she is lonely and Colin forgets that he is sick.

I know it's getting late and I will have to wake up early for school, but I cannot stop reading. Mary and

her friend Dickon form a plan to take Colin into their secret garden. They know that everyone thinks he is much too sick to leave his room, but they are sure that the garden will make him better. And when they open the garden door and push his wheelchair through, Colin cries out *"Mary! Dickon! I shall get well! I shall live forever and ever!"*

I close the book and turn off my light. *The Secret Garden* is a story that's definitely not real. Nothing like that could really happen and nobody lives forever. But when I'm reading it, the story still seems true. Mrs. Shepherd said it was her favorite book as a child. And even now, when she talks about my garden, she feels better. Maybe I can plant ivy and purple crocuses and then the birds will come. I can make a fence with a gate and a lock and a key. And when the garden is ready, we can bring Mrs. Shepherd to see it. *I see my chocolate cherry tomatoes,* she'll say. *And my purple beans climbing up the wall.*

Chapter Six

The First Day of School

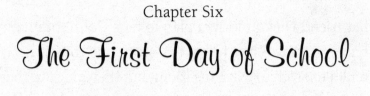

The sky is barely light when we leave for school. Mom holds Ken's hand and I walk ahead by myself. When we pass Laura's house, I think of ringing the doorbell to see if she can walk with us, but the house looks dark, and the dog is in front of the door.

A crossing guard wearing an orange vest greets us when we reach the crosswalk in front of the building. "My name's Ray," he says. "And I'm pleased to meet you."

We tell him our names.

"Anna and Ken. You two are early

today. Good idea on the first day of school." He holds his arms out and we cross the street.

"You can go now," I tell Mom.

Mom's white blouse looks orange in the early-morning light. The wind is blowing her hair, so she holds it in a ponytail with one hand. I think she wants to hug us, but since Dad took us to school last year and the year before, she's not sure what American parents do. The only other people are two teachers talking by the fence. "Have good day," Mom says.

"Bye," I say quickly, taking Ken by the hand.

I help him find 107 painted in white on the blacktop. I find 207. We stand by our classroom numbers and wait. The breeze is cool and I shiver in my thin sweater. Ken looks so small and lonely. I run over and tag him. "You're it," I say. I run slowly on purpose so he can tag me back.

Another kid comes over and joins the game. His

name is Daniel, and he's in Ken's class. In a few minutes Ken forgets all about me.

More and more kids are coming. Three yellow buses pull up and the kids pour out, shouting and running to see their friends. Suddenly someone shouts, "Anna!"

There is Laura in purple pants with a striped shirt. Her hair is flying all over and her cheeks are sunburned. She runs over and grabs my hand. "I knew I'd find you."

"Are you in 207?" I ask.

She nods. "Mr. Ellis."

We stand close together, waiting for the bell to ring. "How was Michigan?" I ask.

"We went tubing."

"What's that?"

"You get in an inner tube and a boat pulls you really fast. It's scary, but it's fun." She pulls up her shirt and her stomach is covered with tiny red blisters. "I got poison ivy in your backyard." She pulls her shirt back down. "It's super itchy. My mom's taking me to the doctor after school."

"Maybe you got it in Michigan," I say.

Laura shakes her head. "I already had it in the car on the way there."

Mr. Ellis has a big head and a big stomach. His voice is loud, but it's not shouting. He welcomes us to third grade which he says is a lot different from second. That's why we are on the second floor with the older kids.

Then Mr. Ellis holds up an empty yogurt container. "What could this be used for?" he asks.

Mom uses those for leftovers, but I don't want to say something that other kids might think is dumb, so I don't raise my hand.

"You could put water in it for your cat to drink," Laura says. "That's what we do."

"A flower pot," a boy named Matthew says.

"A cereal bowl," someone says.

Mr. Ellis is putting all the ideas on the board. He's

water bowl
flower pot
cereal bowl

writing fast so his letters are messy, but we can still read most of the words. Then he explains that our theme for the year is the three Rs. Does anyone know what that might stand for?

One girl says "Reading, writing, and arithmetic," but I think only one of those words starts with R.

"Reduce, Reuse, Recycle," Mr. Ellis finally tells us. "So are these ideas on the board reducing, reusing, or recycling?" he asks.

I raise my hand. "Reusing."

Mr. Ellis nods. "Does anyone know what *reduce* means?"

I know, but I don't think I should keep raising my hand. A girl named Allison says "use less."

Mr. Ellis nods again. "How could we reduce the number of yogurt containers we use?"

Nobody has any ideas.

"What is yogurt made out of?" he asks.

"Milk," a girl says.

"So presumably, we could make our own yogurt out of milk, and then we would not have to make it in plastic containers. And we will do exactly that next week."

"I hate yogurt," Laura whispers.

"Girls," Mr. Ellis says. "Save your private conversation for later."

My cheeks feel hot. Laura was whispering, not me, but Mr. Ellis said *girls* to the two of us. I stare at the top of my desk and wish I were still in Mrs. Mallory's class in second grade at Sutton. She knew I was her reader girl, and when Suzanne whispered to me, she didn't care.

Mr. Ellis holds the yogurt container up again. "And now that we know how to reduce and reuse, how can we recycle this container?"

"Put it into the green bin," says a boy.

Mr. Ellis hands the container to a boy in the front row and asks him to find the little recycling symbol. It has a number 4 next to it, so Mr. Ellis says it's okay to put the empty container into the green recycling bin. "Which of these options would be the best?" he asks.

I think reusing is best because it's fun to use things in a new way. But Mr. Ellis says reducing is best for the environment because then there is less waste overall.

After that we break into groups and go around to different stations, trying to think of ways to reduce, reuse, or recycle things like egg cartons and empty milk jugs. The egg cartons would be perfect for sprouting seeds. We write that down.

The day goes by fast, and by the time the last bell rings, I think third grade will be okay.

Chapter Seven

A Map and a Treasure

It rains a lot over the next few weeks, and the weather turns cool. I look out at the backyard from our kitchen, and everything has turned to mud. When Laura comes over, we're not sure what to play. She asks if we have any board games, but we don't. I show her the postmark collection and the map of the United States.

"We want to add more countries," I say. "Want to make a map of the whole world?"

"How?" Laura asks.

We sit down at the computer and I pull up a world map. I open the cabinet under the sink and take out a brown paper bag. "We could use this." Laura watches me cut one side of the bag and around the bottom. I unfold it and smooth the brown paper out on the table.

"You know how to use everything," she says. "Just like Mr. Ellis." She runs her hand over the brown paper. "I'm bad at drawing."

I get the can of markers off the kitchen counter. Then I look at the world map on the screen and try to draw it onto the brown paper. But I make Africa and Australia too big. Everything is lopsided, and China doesn't fit.

"This is really hard." Laura looks around. "Let's play something else."

Laura always seems so quick to give up. But she's right. The map looks nothing like the one on the screen.

"We can make it into a map of our own world," I say.

Laura looks doubtful. "What do you mean?"

"A made-up world."

"What's it called?" Laura asks.

"I don't know."

Laura looks out the window. "How about 'Laura and Anna's Secret World'?"

I think for a minute. That name is ordinary. But I like the way it reminds me of *The Secret Garden.* "How about putting our names together?"

"What do you mean?" Laura asks.

"Lauranna," I say.

Laura smiles. "You're smart."

I write *Lauranna* on top of the map in fancy cursive.

Laura scratches her stomach. Then she pulls up her shirt and the scabs are still there. "The doctor gave me some medicine. And she said I better not touch poison ivy ever again."

"You didn't try to touch it."

"She says I have to stay away from gardening."

I look up. "Forever?" I can't imagine what I would do if the doctor told me not to do something that I really wanted to do. And I can't imagine doing the garden without Laura.

She shrugs and looks down at the map. "Let's put our houses next to each other."

I draw two houses in the middle of the map on the biggest continent.

"Can you draw my dog and my cat?" Laura asks.

I put them in front of her house.

"I don't think I could survive without them." Laura tells me how her dog and cat both sleep with her every night. "They love to snuggle under the covers with me." Her face looks smooth and happy when she talks about the animals. "They like me best of everyone in the family."

"How do you know?"

"They won't sleep with David or Andrew," she says.

The phone rings, and it's Laura's mom calling to say she has to come home to go to Andrew's soccer game.

"You could ask your mom if you could stay over here instead," I say.

"My dad says we have to go to support each other." Laura zips up her jacket and pulls up her hood. Her face looks small inside of it. "See you later." She puts her hands in her pockets and walks slowly down the hill.

I go out to the garden. The air is damp, but the rain has stopped. Mud has washed onto some of the stones, and a lot of the weeds that we pulled out have popped back up. I get the shovel and try to dig them out by the roots. I wonder if Laura really means that she can't work on the garden with me anymore. Or does she just mean for now? Sometimes people say forever but they don't really mean it.

My shovel hits something hard that sounds like metal. I move the blade around, trying to find the edges of whatever it is. Finally I get underneath it, push down, and fling the thing out of the ground. When I manage to get off the mud, I see that it looks like a big metal spike.

Ken comes around back. "What's that?"

I hand it to my brother.

"A giant nail!" he says.

"Maybe there are more," I say.

We keep digging around the same spot with the shovel and our fingers, but we don't find anything else except for rocks that Ken thinks are fossils, and a soda can.

I run the giant nail under the water spigot on the side of the house. It has a head like a regular nail and a point on one end. It's very rusty and looks as if it's at least a hundred years old. I can't wait to show it to Laura. *That's antique,* she'll say. I bet she'll want to show it to her mom.

That night, Mrs. Morgan calls to tell Mom that Laura has signed up for the girls' soccer team. The practices have already started, but there are a few spaces left. She wonders if I would like to join. She has all the forms at her house, and Laura's dad is the assistant coach.

"I tell her," Mom says. "Thank you so much."

"I don't like soccer," I say when Mom hangs up.

"Laura's mother is very nice to invite you," Mom says. "You can try, see if you like it."

I shake my head. "I know I don't."

"You never try, so you cannot know."

"I know," I say. "We played it last year." My voice is loud and Mom turns away. She says something in Chinese, but I don't know what.

When I see Laura at recess the next day, she is talking to a girl named Lucy and it turns out they are on the same soccer team. So are Rebecca and Allison. They have practice Mondays, Wednesdays, and Fridays after school, and games on the weekends.

"Our uniforms are really cool," Rebecca says. She unzips her jacket to show me. The shirt is white with maroon stripes. On the back is the number nine and it says "Rockets" in cursive. Rebecca is number nine, Allison is four, and Laura is fourteen.

"Why don't you join?" Laura asks. "It's not too late."

"I'm not good at soccer," I say.

"That's okay. My dad'll teach you."

"After you left, I was digging in the garden, and I found this really giant nail," I say. But Laura is busy telling Rebecca that her brother Andrew is going out for the city soccer team. "He's really, really good. My dad says all the coaches are watching him."

"How old is he?" Lucy asks.

"In sixth grade," she says. "He's a forward."

Lucy and Rebecca are really interested in Laura's brother. They want to know what number he has on his shirt and how many goals he scored in the last game.

"You won't believe what I found in our backyard," I say. "I think it's an antique."

But nobody is listening.

I go over to the fence and look out at the street. I wish I was still at Sutton. There was no soccer team there, and we just played whatever we wanted.

I crouch down, pick up a few pebbles, and toss them gently. I throw one up, scoop up the others, and then catch the rock. It's a game Mom taught me when I was little.

"That's just like jacks," Laura says, stooping next to me. "Without a ball."

I keep on tossing the pebbles.

"I was talking to my aunt on the phone last night, and she said she can give us a raised garden bed all to ourselves. We can plant whatever we want." She looks at me. "And there's definitely no poison ivy there."

I scoop up all the pebbles. I don't want to plant Mrs. Shepherd's seeds in Indiana where I can't watch them grow. And I don't want to give up on my backyard garden.

When I don't say anything, Laura tucks in her shirt. "And with soccer, I won't really have much time."

"I want to plant the seeds in my backyard," I say. My voice is sharp.

"Hey, Laura," Rebecca shouts. "Want to play?" She has the soccer ball between her feet.

Laura stands up. The other girls are still huddled together. "Want to kick the soccer ball with us?"

I shake my head.

She smooths out her shirt and heads toward them. I want to say, *Wait, we're friends. We have a garden and a map of a world called Lauranna. And I found a giant nail in our backyard that's a real antique. Do you want to come over after school so I can show it to you?* But the lump in my throat is so big that my voice will not come out.

Chapter Eight

A Note

Every day at recess, Laura, Rebecca, Lucy, and Allison dribble the soccer ball. Sometimes other kids join too. Laura always asks me if I want to play, but I don't. Rebecca is a really fast runner, and Lucy is good at kicking. Allison can keep up pretty well. But Laura has a clumsy way of running. Once she trips over the ball and falls forward. I see Rebecca look at Allison and roll her eyes. But Laura doesn't seem to notice.

Mr. Ellis believes in homework. Lots of it. We have math story problems every day. In social studies, we have to memorize all the states in the United States so that we can label a blank map by heart and put in all the capital cities. Mom helps me make flash cards and we go through them over and over, but no matter how many times we review, I always miss Bismarck, North Dakota; Boise, Idaho; and Cheyenne, Wyoming. After an hour, I am crying.

"Sometimes take a break is good," Mom says. "You can go play with Laura."

"I don't want to play with her," I say. My voice cracks.

Mom puts her arm around my shoulders. "Sometimes a break from friend is good too."

"She has other friends," I say, rubbing my nose with my sleeve.

Mom tries to pull me close. "Other friends does not mean you are not a friend too."

"Yes it does," I say, standing up and running out into the backyard.

I grab the shovel from the garage and start turning over the dirt in our garden as fast as I can. The soil is dry now and the top layer is hard, but if I put my foot on the blade of the shovel and push down, I can do it. I make my way across the back of the garden near the border, putting in the shovel, pushing down on it with all my weight, and turning over the dirt. Each time I move the shovel, I say the name of a state and its capital. *Frankfurt, Kentucky; Boise, Idaho; Springfield, Illinois; Cheyenne, Wyoming; North Dakota . . . what is the capital of North Dakota?* I push the shovel down. *Bismarck.* When Mom calls me in for dinner, I have the soil in most of the garden turned over and I know every single capital city.

First thing in the morning, Mr. Ellis gives each of us a blank map. I fill it in with the names of the states and the capitals as fast as I can. When I am done, I see that everyone else is still working. I want to read, but then they will know that I finished before everyone else, so I keep staring at my paper.

Finally Mr. Ellis collects the maps. When Laura looks up, her face is red, even her ears, and her map is half blank. I want to tell her, *It's okay, Mr. Ellis said he's going to do a retest next week. You can use my flashcards to study.* But Laura has her head down.

When we get into groups to work on our recycling project, Laura is not in the room. I think maybe she went to the bathroom, but after fifteen minutes she is still not back. When I ask Mr. Ellis, he says she didn't feel well so he sent her to the nurse's office. She does not come back for the rest of the school day. I cannot stop thinking about Laura. She always asks me if I want to play soccer with the other girls but I never do. Maybe that hurts her feelings. But when she wants to quit working on the garden, it hurts my feelings too.

Our group is working on composting. The compost

can is full of apple cores and banana peels. Now someone has to take it out to the big bin.

"It stinks," Matthew says, holding his nose.

"I'll do it," I say, taking the can and heading out.

The sun is bright but the air is cool. I walk around the edge of the baseball field to the compost bin. I open the lid and empty the can. Inside are lots of worms. Laura would love to watch them moving around on the apple cores and orange peels. She probably knows all about worms, like what they eat and what different kinds there are. I look down the block. If you turn left and go down the hill, you get to Laura's house. Maybe now she's snuggling in bed with Lily and Liliana. She looked so upset after the blank map quiz. Maybe she is sobbing into her pillow.

I head back into the classroom and wait for the bell to ring.

When I get home, I go up to my room. I still don't have a desk, so I sit on the edge of the bed, open my book bag, and take out my notebook and a pencil. I should start on my homework, but instead I write a note.

> Dear Laura,
> I hope you feel better soon. Here are flash cards in case you want to study the capitals.
> Your friend,
> Anna.

I reread my note. It doesn't sound right. I don't even know what I want to say. I tear up the note and start over.

> Dear Laura,
> I hope you feel better.

What else should I write? When I watch Laura play- ing soccer at recess she looks worried. And when she's writing or reading, she looks worried too. I want to tell her, *It's okay, Lily and Liliana are waiting for you at home. We have almost the same birthday, remember? We have a land of our own called Lauranna. And we have our very own secret garden. I'll make sure there's no more poison ivy anywhere.*

Then I remember Laura's sweaty face and the poison ivy blisters on her stomach. Maybe I should write her that if she doesn't want to work on the garden, there are lots of other things we can do. But instead I write:

> Here are some flash cards that I made to study for the test. Maybe you would like to use them.
> Your friend,
> Anna

Around the border I make little cat and dog faces. Then I fold the note and tape it shut. I could take it down to Laura's house and give it to her. But what would I say? I still don't want to join the soccer team and I still don't want to plant our seeds at her aunt's farm. And maybe Laura doesn't want my flash cards. Maybe she doesn't want me.

I ball up the note and toss it into the garbage can.

Chapter Nine

Poison Ivy

When we get to the Shepherds', Mrs. Shepherd is lying on the sofa and Mr. Shepherd is sitting in his wheelchair right beside her.

"Aren't we glad to see you," he says. "Where's Ken?"

"He spent the night at a friend's," I say. I take the big rusty nail out of my bag to show it to Mr. Shepherd.

He turns it this way and

that. "That's called a railroad spike, to keep the railroad tracks in place."

"Do you think there was a railroad track in our backyard?"

He scratches his head. "Could be. Or could be someone was using that railroad spike for something else. They come in handy, for digging, hammering. Things like that." He gives it back to me. "I'd hold on to it."

Mrs. Shepherd sits up. "How's your garden coming along?"

"I got most of the soil turned over."

"That's not easy," she says. "Remember, Sylvan, all those bushes and rocks? Then we added compost." She takes a deep breath. "It surely was a process." She sits back against the pillow. "But was it ever worth it. Sweet warm tomatoes, crispy green beans." I can tell she is in another world as she talks. "Did I give you the seeds for the chocolate cherries?"

I nod.

"Sweet as candy."

"The honeysuckles are hard to dig out," I say. "And the weeds keep popping up."

"You've got that right," Mr. Shepherd says. "Some of them are as big as trees. Our neighbor over there, Mr. Smith, he helped us on occasion."

"My neighbor Laura was helping me, but now she . . ." I think of telling the Shepherds about the soccer team and new friends and how Laura and I hardly talk at school these days. Then I say, "She got poison ivy."

Mrs. Shepherd nods. "Some people get it bad. I know each plant has its right to this world, same as you and I. But the use of that one is hard to understand." She closes her eyes for a minute and I can see that all this talking tires her out. "Let me tell you, it is possible to rid an area of poison ivy. First, learn exactly what it looks like. Three spiky leaves and a red stem. Sometimes it's a vine and sometimes it's a freestanding plant. Each time you see it, put a plastic bag over your hands and dig it out, roots and all. Soon enough, it'll take its vines elsewhere. Plants can be stubborn, but eventually they learn when they're not wanted."

Mrs. Shepherd closes her eyes again. Mr. Shepherd puts his finger to his lips, and I follow his wheelchair into the kitchen. "Let me pour you a glass of lemonade, Anna," he says. "Fresh squeezed this morning." He puts ice into the glasses and pours the lemonade on top. "Mrs. Shepherd has spent the past two weeks cleaning out every single closet. I keep telling her she's tiring herself out, but she seems to want to get everything in order." He sighs. "She's talking about how the house is too much for us now." He takes a sip of lemonade. "I think she knows something we don't." I look into his eyes, which are cloudy and gray. "She wants to move into one of those high-rises—you know, with a river view. She says that way when she's gone, I'll have something beautiful to look at and I won't feel so alone." His eyes tear up. "But you never know. I may be the one to go first."

Mom is cleaning the kitchen counter. "Mrs. Shepherd thinks ahead," she whispers.

"I suppose sometimes that's good," Mr. Shepherd says. "And sometimes it isn't." He clears his throat. "She's not been eating well these days. Says her stomach's all topsy-turvy, but she won't let me take her to the doctor."

"Topsy-turvy?" Mom says.

"You know, unsettled."

Mom nods. I know she is repeating *topsy-turvy* over

and over in her head so she can remember it.

"Only thing she likes is your soup." Mr. Shepherd turns to me. "She found a few tools for you, Anna." He points to a box, and inside is a spade, a trowel with three prongs, and a dandelion digger.

"Thank you," I say, putting the railroad spike into the box.

When Mrs. Shepherd wakes up, she has some soup that Mom made with ginger and chicken.

"I don't know what we would do without you and your mother," Mrs. Shepherd says. She takes tiny sips of the hot broth. "With our nieces far away, and both of us getting so old . . ." She looks out the window. "See that bird there on the balcony? That's a red-headed woodpecker."

"My neighbor Laura knows about birds. Her uncle is a bird-watcher."

Mrs. Shepherd nods. "Some people are bird people. Now, I like birds, but I can't say I'm an expert."

Mr. Shepherd gets a book off the shelf. "Take this home, Anna." He rummages in his desk drawer. "And this, too." He hands me binoculars. "Great for spotting hummingbirds."

"Don't you need them?" I ask.

"These eyes of mine are too cloudy," he says. "You can come back and tell us what you saw, and that'll be better than trying to see for ourselves."

Mrs. Shepherd finishes her soup. "They may take a little while to attract, but once you do, hummingbirds can be your best friends. They're great pollinators, just like bees and dragonflies." She shows me a calendar from last year. "See here, Anna, I have everything written down that I did in the garden each month. I thought maybe you could follow along. You know, a kind of guide from one year to the next."

Mom packs up her bucket and cleaning supplies. "We will be back next Saturday," Mom says. "Or we can come before if you call."

"I've got the number in here," Mr. Shepherd says, pointing to his forehead.

Mom holds her bucket in one hand and my hand in the other, and together we walk to the bus stop.

"Can we start a compost pile?" I ask.

Mom doesn't understand.

"We could save all our potato skins and banana peels and apple cores. Then we can make a pile in the backyard that will turn into soil."

Mom nods. "In China, my grandmother buries everything under the ground. Even chicken fat. We don't waste. And she had very beautiful flowers."

Mom never told me about her grandmother before. "Does she grow vegetables?"

Mom nods. "She has tomatoes and small cabbages. But mostly she likes flowers."

"What kind?" I ask.

Mom's eyes look far away. "I don't know the name in English. Yellow flowers, orange color too. So beautiful. They open in fall."

"We can ask Mrs. Shepherd what they're called," I say.

On the bus, I lean on Mom's shoulder and try to imagine her grandmother's garden in China. I didn't know Mom knew anything about compost or gardening. She never told me before.

When we get home, I go around back. The wind is cold and I pull up my hood to cover my ears. In the corner of the garden in between two rocks is a small green plant. How can something grow when it's freezing? I go closer. Three spiky leaves and a red stem. It must be poison ivy.

I get a plastic bag from the kitchen, cover my hand, and pull the whole thing up, careful not to let any part of it touch my skin. The roots are long and tangled, and they lead me to two more small plants. When I think I got them all, I throw the plants into the garbage can along with the plastic bag. Then I search the whole rest of the garden for poison ivy, but I don't find any more spiky leaves or red stems.

I walk up the hill to the sidewalk and look toward Laura's house. She's probably up in her room with Lily and Liliana. I could walk down and tell her that I got rid of all the poison ivy. I could see if she wants to make a gate for the garden, or a compost bin. I think we have some wood in our garage.

I miss hearing about Laura's pets and her aunt's farm. I miss her soft voice and her hair that flies around her face in the wind. But at school, she is busy talking to Lucy and Rebecca. Maybe she is too busy with soccer and her new friends. Maybe she doesn't miss me at all.

Finally I go in and scrub my hands with dish detergent.

Chapter Ten

A Winter Discovery

The first day of holiday break, Ken wakes me up as soon as the sun rises.

"Look outside!"

My room is strangely bright. I turn toward the window, and snow covers everything. Ken and I bundle up and head out.

"Let's make a snowman," Ken says, handing me a snowball. The snow is perfect for packing, and we roll the ball until it's so heavy, we can't move it anymore. Then we start on the second ball, and finally we make the head. I find rocks for the eyes, and mom gives us a carrot for the nose.

"He needs a scarf," Ken says, taking off his scarf and tying it onto the snowman.

"It's a snow-woman," I say, finding twigs for hair.

"How do you know?" Ken asks.

"She told me," I say, throwing a snowball at Ken. He throws one back. Soon we are covered with wet snow. After our snowball fight, Ken gets cold, but I'm not ready to go in. I head around back.

Every honeysuckle branch has an inch of snow on it, and the rock border of the garden is hidden. I poke around with my boots until I find a stone, and then the next one and the next one until I make footprints along the border. When I get to the back by the bushes, I turn around. What is that moving in the leaves? I look more closely, and there, partly covered by the bushes, is a baby rab-

bit. Its sides are moving in and out, and its black eyes look terrified. My stomach flips. What should I do? Where is the mother? The little rabbit might freeze outside in the snow.

The small hill to the sidewalk is slippery, but I dig in my boots and grab the honeysuckle branches until I'm up. Then I run down the hill as fast as I can, past the house with the white shades and the one next to it with the blue shutters. When I get to the mailbox with the cat painted on it, I turn down the brick walkway, breathing hard.

Laura's brother answers the door. "Is Laura home?" I ask.

"Laur," he calls. His voice is deep.

She comes down the stairs wearing basketball shorts and a T-shirt. Her face is red and sweaty.

"There's a baby rabbit!" I say.

Laura pulls a pair of jeans over her shorts, grabs her jacket, and slips on her boots, and we start running up the hill. "Where'd you find it?"

"In the back of the garden. I'll show you."

We balance on the stones until we get to the edge of the bushes. The rabbit is exactly where I left it, its sides moving in and out so fast that it's trembling.

Laura stoops down. "Poor little bunny. How'd you get so lost?"

The rabbit moves its nose.

"The mom must be somewhere," Laura says. "And brothers and sisters. Rabbits have lots of babies at once."

We start searching in the honeysuckles around the garden, and in the ivy that's covered with snow. Then we go down into the gully and up the other side, but there are no other rabbits anywhere.

"What should we do?" I ask.

Laura looks at the sun. "I think we should leave the rabbit where it is as long as we can to see if the mother comes back. But if it's still here at night, it'll get too cold."

"Then what?"

"When I was on my aunt's farm, my cousin and I found a baby rabbit. We made it a nest in a box and fed it."

"Did it survive?"

Laura shakes her head and her hair flies out from under her hood. "But that doesn't mean this one won't." She stoops down to look at the bunny again.

"You're a little fighter, aren't you." Laura's voice has a firmness that I never heard before.

The rabbit moves its ears as if it's listening.

We go into our garage and find an empty box. Then we go around the backyard collecting leaves and grass to make a little nest in the corner of the box.

"Want to go inside for a while?" I ask, shivering.

Our kitchen is warm and steamy. Laura takes a deep breath. "Smells good in here." Mom is putting the lid on our big pot that has three levels. "What's that?"

"A steamer pot," I say. Then I tell Mom that we found a baby rabbit.

She looks worried. "A wild animal can be sick."

"I think it just got lost some-how," Laura says, with confidence.

Mom turns the flame down on the stove.

"What's a steamer pot?" Laura asks.

"You can cook many things at the same time," Mom says.

"Like a three-story house," Laura says.

Mom nods. "We can make different . . ." Mom looks at me for the word in English.

"Dumplings," I say.

Mom gives us each a bowl with three dumplings and some cabbage. Laura wrinkles her nose, but after she tastes a dumpling, she smiles. "These are good." But she doesn't taste the cabbage.

I tip my bowl to drink the hot broth.

"I don't really like most vegetables," Laura says, putting her bowl into the sink with the cabbage untouched.

Just before sunset, we walk along the rocks to where the rabbit was. Laura walks ahead and I carry the box. It's hard to find the bunny in the near dark, but then Laura sees something move.

"You're a good little bunny," she says. "You'll be okay." She touches the rabbit gently between its ears.

Then she puts her fingers underneath its belly and lifts it carefully into the box. The rabbit scurries to the corner and waits, still breathing fast.

"Let's take it to my house," Laura says. "We can keep it in the garage."

"What do we feed it?"

Laura is thinking. "Cow's milk is bad for baby rabbits. They're supposed to get dog or cat milk."

"Where do we get that?"

"I bet my mom'll take us to the pet store."

We carry the box between the two of us, trying not to jostle the baby rabbit. When we get to the garage, we put it on the floor. Laura finds an old screen leaning against the wall and puts it on top of the box. "In case he decides to jump," she says.

All the pet stores are closed. Laura's mother thinks the rabbit might not survive without milk until the morning. Laura pulls her eyebrows together the way she does when she's concentrating. "Maybe Aunt Clare has some. They rescue baby animals all the time."

Laura picks up the phone to call her aunt, and in less than half an hour, we are on the way to Indiana with the bunny in a box between us on the back seat.

Chapter Eleven

Indiana

Once we get off the highway, the road narrows and we can hardly see through the windows. Freezing rain hits the windshield.

"I've driven through blizzards," Laura's mom says. "A little sleet won't stop us."

It's almost ten when we finally pull into a long drive-way. At the end is a small white house, and behind it is the barn. "That's where Pooky stays," Laura says. "The horse."

Our baby rabbit is huddled in a corner of the box with his eyes wide open. Laura takes off her jacket to cover the box. "Rabbits can get sick if they get too

wet," she says. We take him into the kitchen.

Aunt Clare is taller and thinner than Laura's mom, but she has the same narrow face and blue eyes.

"I've heard about you, Anna," she says, taking my hand in both of hers. She already has the cat milk defrosting in the sink. "I keep this on hand just in case there's something to rescue." She hugs Laura. "We know a lot about that, don't we, Laura. Squirrels, raccoons, birds. You name it, we've found it." She looks into the box. "Poor thing is scared to death." She heats the milk in the microwave for a few seconds, then squeezes a dropper to fill it.

"You girls want to give it a try?" she asks.

I have no idea how to feed the baby rabbit and I'm scared to try.

Laura takes the dropper from her aunt. "Here, little bunny, have some nice warm milk." She puts the

dropper into the rabbit's mouth and squeezes it slowly. Some of the milk runs down into his fur, but he does swallow about half. Laura fills the dropper again. "You're a big mess," she says to the rabbit. "Let's go a little slower now."

It takes about an hour, but finally the rabbit seems full. Aunt Clare thinks we should keep the box in the barn. "The little rabbit will feel more comfortable out there," she says. "He's used to being outside."

"What should we name it?" Laura asks as she picks up the box.

The rabbit is a big gooey mess with milk in its fur. "Goo?" I say.

Laura smiles. "Goo Morgan Wang."

Aunt Clare gives me a big flashlight. "Watch your step out there," she says. "Looks like some of that rain has turned to ice."

We make our way to the barn. When I open the door, the horse stomps its feet. "We brought you a friend, Pooky," Laura says.

We put the box on a high shelf. "Up high is safer," Laura says.

"Good night, Goo," I say.

"Sleep well, Little Bunny." Laura pets him between his ears. Then she puts the screen onto the box, takes my hand, and leads me back to the house, where we'll spend the night.

Aunt Clare has a nightgown for each of us and extra toothbrushes. We sleep in the room that has bunk beds. I choose the bottom bunk.

Laura turns over and the whole bed shakes. I wonder how I'll ever fall asleep without Ken and my parents and a book to read. I lie down on my side the way I usually do, but my head is spinning and I have a stomachache.

Laura hangs her head down so I see her face upside down. "How are you doing down there?"

"I've never slept away from home. Except when I was little we went to China, but I was with my parents."

"I've slept away from home a bunch of times," Laura

says. "At Girl Scout camp, and here, and at my grandparents' in Kentucky. The only things I miss are Lily and Liliana."

"You're lucky," I say. "The rest of my family lives really far away."

Laura puts her head back up. "Your family is really peaceful compared to mine."

I think about that for a minute. I haven't spent time at Laura's house, but she says her brothers fight all the time and her parents, too. "Your family is more adventurous," I say. "My mom would never drive me to Indiana at night in the rain for a baby bunny."

"I hope he doesn't die," Laura says.

I close my eyes and think of the bunny in the corner of his box with his sides fluttering. "Do you think he might die in one night?"

I hear Laura take a deep breath. "He's a fighter."

In the middle of the night, I open my eyes, and Laura has her jacket on and a bottle in her hands. "I'm going to check on Goo," she whispers. "I think he might need more milk. Want to come?"

I sit up. The bed is warm and it's pitch dark outside. I don't really want to get up, but I put on my shoes and pull my jacket over my pajamas. Laura shines the flashlight on the path, and we head out to the barn.

Goo is leaning against the side of the box, completely still. "Is he still alive?" I whisper.

Laura puts her head close. "I don't hear anything."

The horse snorts in his stall, startling me. "It's okay, Pooky," Laura says. Then she touches the bunny. "He's still warm," she says. "And breathing." She pets the top of his head and he moves his ears. She fills the dropper. At first Goo doesn't want the milk and it runs onto his fur. But Laura keeps trying to squeeze the dropper slowly, and finally Goo takes a little.

"Do you want to try?" Laura asks.

What if I give him too much milk and he chokes? The barn is cold and I shiver in the night air.

"It's not hard," Laura says. She is holding the dropper, ready to show me. "You just put it into the side of his mouth and squeeze."

The light from the flashlight shines on Laura's face. Her cheeks are pink from the cold, and her eyes are begging. She really wants to teach me.

At first I squeeze too hard, but then I slow down and watch him swallow. I refill the dropper five times, and most of the milk goes into Goo's mouth.

"You did it," Laura says.

"Thanks for teaching me," I say. "And thanks for waking up. Goo might have died by morning."

"Thanks to you, too," Laura says.

"For what?"

"For coming to get me when you found him."

We climb back into our beds, but I don't fall asleep for a long time. I think about Goo in his box, and Mom and Dad and Ken at home, and Laura in the bed above mine. When we were working on the garden, Laura seemed so quick to give up. And when we were making our map, too. But with Goo, she is determined to help him fight for his life. And she is determined to include me.

In the morning, Laura says Goo took two more feedings during the night.

"I didn't hear you get up," I say.

"I tried to be quiet," Laura says.

"You hardly slept, then."

But Laura doesn't look tired. "I love taking care of animals," she says. "It's my favorite thing in the whole world."

I think about that for a minute. "I think I'm more of a plant person."

Laura smiles. "Plants and animals go together."

Then I tell Laura about *The Secret Garden.* "There are birds and rabbits and foxes and flowers and ivy, all mixed together. And this girl Mary, and her friends Dickon and Colin." I look down. "I was thinking we could try to make our garden like that."

Laura is really listening. "I'm not good at reading fat books. But if we read it out loud, I'll understand it."

We spend the afternoon exploring the farm. Laura shows me the place in the barn where she found the family of mice, and the hollow log with the opossum. Next she shows me the garden. There are eight raised beds with icy paths in between, and a fence around the whole thing to keep the deer out. In the corner, there's a pile of mulch and a compost bin.

"Wow, this is a professional garden," I say. I think of my backyard with the honeysuckles all around and new weeds popping up each day. How will our garden ever look like this one? I wonder for a second if we really should plant our seeds here, where everything is in perfect order. I look at Laura, and she seems to know what I'm thinking. "Mrs. Shepherd is really happy about our backyard garden." I swallow. "Every time I see her, she asks about our progress."

Laura is listening. "I think old people like to know . . . I mean, they want their things to keep going." Laura slips on the ice and grabs on to my jacket. "My aunt said she can give us some asparagus shoots." She wrinkles her nose. "Even though I don't like it."

"I bet everyone will like our chocolate cherry tomatoes." I smile.

By the time we go back home to Ohio, Goo has had five feedings, and we have enough milk to last until Monday, when Laura's mom says she will get more milk at the pet store.

Chapter Twelve

Freedom

By Christmas, Goo is almost twice as big as he was when we found him. And by Chinese New Year, he looks practically grown.

"Let's give him some carrots," I say, as we head into my house. "To celebrate the year of the Ox."

Mom is sitting at our new dining room table with three red envelopes, one for Ken, one for me, and one for Laura. "*Xin nian kuai le,*" she says, handing Laura one of the envelopes.

"That means happy new year," I say.

Laura blushes. "Thank you," she says, smiling.

"We get a red envelope every year," I say.

Mom nods. "This is our tradition in China, called *hong bao.*"

Laura tries to repeat, but it sounds like *honk bow.*

"Very good," Mom says.

Laura feels the envelope. "What's inside?"

"Open it," Mom says. "You will see."

Laura and I open our envelopes at the same time. "Thank you," Laura says again, holding the chocolate coins in the palm of her hand. She puts them back into the envelope. "I'm going to show my mom."

I open the fridge and take out a carrot. "Goo's Chinese New Year gift," I say, breaking it in half and giving the top to Laura as we head back out.

On the way to Laura's, I glance down at our garden. The weather has been too cold and wet to work outside, plus with Goo, and Laura's soccer practices, there hasn't been much time. We still don't have the raised beds ready.

From the sidewalk, it looks more like a mud hole than a garden.

"We need to start working on the raised beds," I say, pointing to the garden.

Laura doesn't say anything,

We let Goo out of his box every day to explore. His nose twitches a lot and his ears move back and forth. He eats weeds in the backyard, and we give him lettuce, carrots, and apple slices.

"I'll ask my aunt when we should let him go," Laura says.

The woods are big and scary. "What if a cat comes and attacks him?" I ask. "Maybe we should just keep him as a pet."

Laura shakes her head. "He wouldn't be happy."

❊ ❊ ❊

Aunt Clare says we should let Goo out for longer and longer periods of each day. Then, when the weather warms up, we can set him free.

Each time we let him out, Goo goes farther away from his box. He follows his nose, sniffing in the bushes and grass and thistle weeds. He ventures to the edge of the driveway. Then one day, after we let him out, we go into Laura's house garage to get a jump rope, and when we get back, Goo is gone. We search all over the gully and the hillside, and even down the street, but we don't see a gray rabbit with a white tail.

"What if he's lost?" I say.

"Rabbits don't get lost." Laura looks down and her hair falls over her face. "I think he decided it was time to leave."

Laura's eyes are watery. I touch her arm. "Do you want to go into your house and play cards?" I ask.

We go inside and play concentration on Laura's living room floor. Then she teaches me how to play war and twenty-one. After a while, we go into the kitchen to get a drink of water. Laura looks out the back window. "I can't stop worrying about Goo."

"I know. Me either."

"I wonder if we'll ever see him again."

"I hope so," I say, trying to spot a gray rabbit with a white tail on the hillside. "Want to go plant the lettuce seeds?" I ask. "Mrs. Shepherd said it's a cool-weather crop."

When Laura pulls her eyebrows together, I tell her about pulling out the poison ivy. "Mrs. Shepherd told me how to get rid of it. Each time I see it, I dig it out by the roots. I think it's all gone." I look at Laura. "But if you're worried about it, we can do something else."

Laura wipes her hands on her jeans and we head out.

❄ ❄ ❄

We take turns using the railroad spike to break up the clods of dirt.

"Do you think this railroad spike is a real antique?" I ask.

Laura looks at it. "I'll ask my mom. It sure looks old."

After the dirt is smooth, we find small stones to mark the section for the lettuce. Then we make little lines with our fingers, sprinkle the lettuce seeds in the groves, cover them up with a little bit of fine soil, and pat them down.

"Do you think we should water them?" Laura asks.

The air is damp. "Rain is coming," I say.

I mark the ends of the rows with twigs so we'll remember where we planted the seeds. Then I look around our garden. It looks so small and bare. I wonder if it'll ever look like Mary's secret garden with vines and purple flowers and vegetables all around.

I walk down the hill with Laura. The sky is gray and the air is chilly. "It'll be weird to go to sleep without thinking about Goo in his box," Laura says. "Sometimes I hear owls at night and I think one could swoop down and kill a baby rabbit."

"Goo isn't that small anymore."

Laura nods. We look down the street. "I hope he knows to stay away from cars."

"And cats," I say.

"I hope Goo can find other rabbit friends."

"I hope he finds things to eat."

"I hope he has a good life," Laura says. She's trying hard not to cry.

"Maybe we'll see him around." I look toward the gully.

"Maybe," she says, heading down the hill. "See you tomorrow."

We both keep saying bye until I can't see Laura anymore.

Chapter Thirteen

A Storm

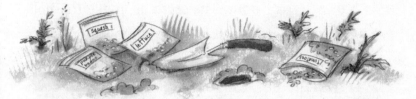

$\mathcal{I}$t rains for three days in a row, and the garden floods. Mrs. Shepherd says that a good soaking never hurts, but I think the lettuce seeds probably washed out to the street and down the sewer.

"In that case you'll have to replant," she says. "The weather is one of those things in life we cannot control. I've saved some egg cartons for you, Anna. Thought

you could start the tomato plants about now." She puts her head back to rest. "Then, once they've grown their real leaves and the ground is warm, you can set them out. The secret is, make the hole deep. They'll grow more roots right out of the stem."

I want to ask Mrs. Shepherd about how we can attract hummingbirds, but I know that talking tires her out. She goes to lie down on the sofa. Ken and I sit on the living room floor looking through the box of magazines. We both like the pictures that have a list of objects hidden somewhere. In the last one, I find a rabbit hidden among the leaves in a tree.

"That's Goo," I tell Ken.

He smiles. "Rabbits can't climb trees."

"Maybe ours can."

❋ ❋ ❋

Lightning fills the room and the thunder comes fast. "Storm's right on us this time," Mr. Shepherd says. He explains how you can tell the distance you are from a storm by the time between the lightning and the thunder.

"That's cool," Ken says, counting two seconds between the next bolt of lightning and the thunder.

"I always did like a good storm," Mrs. Shepherd says. "Long as I'm not out in it and nobody gets hurt."

"I wonder how our rabbit is doing," I say.

"Animals know how to hide," Mr. Shepherd says. "Your rabbit will be just fine. I'm sure he found a hollow tree stump to wait it out."

"I don't know. Goo didn't have a mother to teach him stuff."

Mrs. Shepherd motions for me to sit by her on the sofa. "Some things are instinct, Anna." She is talking so quietly, I can hardly hear. "Your bunny will know how to hide from the rain even if nobody taught him."

"Do you know which flowers attract hummingbirds?" I ask.

Mrs. Shepherd thinks for a minute. "Foxglove and lupine."

I get a piece of paper and a pencil and Mrs. Shepherd tells me again. Mr. Shepherd says when the weather warms up, he can give me some of the plants they have in their backyard. "Good to separate them," he says. "Thin them out a bit."

The wind is whipping the tree branches around and the rain is blowing sideways, hitting the window. Ken grabs my arm, and suddenly the room is dark.

"Power out," Mr. Shepherd says, wheeling himself over to the drawer and getting one big flashlight and two little ones. "Here, one for each of you," he says, handing the small ones to us. Mom joins us in the living room.

There is a knock on the door, and Dad steps in. His hair is wet and water is dripping off his jacket. "I was worried about you," he says, taking a package of candles out of his jacket pocket. In his other hand is a box of my favorite snack, Cheddar Cheese Nips.

We light the small candles. Then we help Mrs. Shepherd to the table, and all six of us sit around eating Cheese Nips and watching the candles burn down.

I play with the melted wax, molding it with my fingers. I roll it into a ball, then pull out a small head and two long ears. Soon it takes the shape of a little bunny.

Chapter Fourteen

A Story

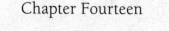

Mr. Ellis gives each of us a blank bound book to write and illustrate a story about anything we want. But before we actually write the story into the book, we're supposed to plan it out. The first step is called brainstorming, Mr. Ellis says. That's when you let your brain wander to find ideas.

"I might write about Lily," Laura says. "My grandma found him when he was just a puppy, tied up to the playground fence."

"You mean somebody tied him up and left him?" Matthew asks.

Laura nods.

"I'm going to write about our vacation in Florida," Simon says. "The waves were taller than me."

"I'm going to write about the soccer finals," Rebecca says.

Mr. Ellis says we should make a list of at least five ideas. Then we're supposed to circle the one we like best, and try to list more details. Kids are writing really fast. Laura seems to have a whole list. But my mind is blank. I write my name, Anna Wang, in fancy cursive, and I draw squiggles around it. I draw flowers around the border of the paper. But my mind won't wander.

Finally I start to write:

One day I got some seeds. And then I thought maybe I could plant a real garden. I got this idea because I read The Secret Garden. I think this might be my favorite book I ever read. I stop writing for a minute. I actually got the seeds before I read the book. I start over.

My mom says when I was a baby I used to love to play with dirt and when I got bigger, I picked her bouquets of little flowers. When we drove places, we passed farms and I wished I lived on one. That's why when I got some seeds, I thought I could make my own garden. Then I read a book called <u>The Secret Garden</u> and my biggest wish in the world is to make a garden like that.

I look up and Mr. Ellis is walking around the room. When he gets to me, I think he might say that I didn't list my ideas, but he doesn't seem to mind. Then I ask if he ever read *The Secret Garden*.

He nods. "One of my favorites." He lets his eyes move over my paragraph. "Glad you've got an idea now, Anna." He goes on to Lucy, who sits next to me.

When the bell rings, it's hard to believe it's already three o'clock. "Want to come over?" I ask Laura.

She nods.

❋ ❋ ❋

After so much rain, everything is clean and bright. Daffodils are blooming in most of the yards, and the grass is green.

"I like dandelions," I say, picking one that is blooming by the edge of the sidewalk.

"I don't see why they're weeds," Laura says. She picks a purple flower. "Violets, too."

Ken finds a weed with white flowers growing out of a crack in the sidewalk.

By the time we get to my house, Ken, Laura, and I have a whole bouquet. We put the flowers into a vase.

"So beautiful," Mom says.

"They're weeds," Laura says.

"Beautiful weeds," Mom says. She takes three *baotse* out of the freezer and puts them into the steamer for our snack.

Laura looks at me. "How do you say 'thank you' in Chinese?"

"*Xie xie,*" I tell her.

Laura turns to my mom. "*Xie xie,*" she tries to say.

"*Bu xie,*" Mom says. "That means 'you're welcome.'"

"What are these buns called?" Laura asks.

"*Baotse,*" I say. "With red bean paste inside."

"I don't like beans," she says.

"These are really sweet. You should try them."

Laura hesitates. "I'm not that good at trying new things."

I think about that for a minute. "I'm not either. Especially things like soccer."

While Mom is steaming the *baotse,* we go out to check on the garden, and sprinkled on the black dirt are tiny green dots.

"Lettuce!" I shout. I can't believe it sprouted so fast!

"Those tiny things?" Laura asks.

We look closely at the soil, trying to decide which green dots are actually lettuce and which are weeds popping up after the rain. I hope none of them are new poison ivy plants.

"It's not really in rows like we planted it," Laura says.

"I guess the rain moved the seeds around."

"Our garden has a mind of its own," Laura says.

Chapter Fifteen

A Setback

I can't believe I slept until almost ten.

"I was wondering when you were going to finally wake up," Ken says.

He wants me to help him with a diorama he's supposed to make for school about a book that he likes. "But I don't like any books," he says.

"That's not true. You've read all the Dr. Seuss books."

Ken is almost in tears. "Those are baby books."

We look at the books on my shelf. "Here, I'll read you the first chapter of this one," I say, taking *Sarah, Plain and Tall* off my shelf. "Then you can read the rest of it by yourself."

We sit together in the new beanbag chair in the living room and I end up reading Ken the whole book.

"I like Caleb best," he says. Ken is thinking for a minute. "I wish their mother didn't die."

"At least they like Sarah."

"And she likes them," Ken says. He decides to put Caleb and the dogs in the diorama. And their house with the flower garden. I help him draw the people, but he cuts everything out and tapes the characters in himself.

After lunch, I go out to the garden. But something looks different. There are lots of holes in the dirt, and many of the lettuce plants have big bites out of their leaves. Some have been eaten all the way down to the ground, leaving only a small green nub. I feel tears come to my eyes. After all the work we did to make the garden, everything is ruined! I wish I'd never tried to make a garden in the first place. First the land had to be cleared, then it turned into a muddy mess, and now when finally the plants started to

grow, they're all eaten up. I wish Mrs. Shepherd were here. She would know what to do.

I run down the hill to get Laura.

"I wonder if it was rabbits," she says as we hurry back to my house. Laura looks closely at the leaves. Then she points to the dirt. "Those are rabbit paw prints."

"How do you know?"

"That's how their feet are, remember?"

"Maybe it was Goo." And then I am crying.

Laura touches the small plants. "I think most of them'll grow back. I'll call my aunt. She'll know what to do."

Aunt Clare says that first we should sprinkle black pepper on the plants that are left. That should keep the rabbits away for the time being. Then when she comes to town on Wednesday, she can bring us some chicken wire to make a small fence around the lettuce bed.

Laura is thinking. "And let's plant some more lettuce outside of the fence for the rabbits."

Laura's idea makes me smile. "Then we can have our salad, and Goo can have his dessert," I say.

Chapter Sixteen
A Birthday Celebration

Laura comes to the door. "One more week," she says.

"Until what?"

"My birthday. And eight days until yours. Want to celebrate together?" Laura's cheeks are flushed. "Do you like ice cream cake?"

I like ice cream cake, but I usually celebrate my birthday with just our family.

"My mom makes this cake with chocolate chip cookies on the bottom and ice cream on top." Laura uses her hands to show me the size of the cake and is talking fast. "We need ten candles on top, one for each year plus one to grow on."

"Where would we have the party?" I ask.

"Our patio?" Laura says.

I look out the back window. The garden is starting to look real now, with wire pro-tecting the lettuce and

the stone border around the edge. Laura's aunt also helped us make raised beds for beans and squash. "How about in our garden?"

Laura opens her eyes wide. "We could move our picnic table out there."

"And we can decorate the table with wildflowers."

"We can make clover necklaces for everyone. This is going to be the best birthday I ever had," Laura says.

"What day should we have it?" I ask, going over to the wall calendar.

"My mom doesn't work on Saturdays."

"My mom cleans the Shepherds' house on Satur-days."

"How about inviting them?" Laura asks.

I think about that for a minute. "Mrs. Shepherd is really weak. I don't think she can go anywhere."

Laura pulls her eyebrows together. "But maybe we can help her into the car. My dad has a van that could fit the wheelchair."

I am about to say that I don't think that would be possible. Mrs. Shepherd can hardly support her own weight, so how could we get her into the car? Then I think of Colin in *The Secret Garden*. "I'll ask my mom," I say. "After she cleans their house, maybe they can come over for a short visit."

"Long enough to eat ice cream cake."

"And see the lettuce plants," I say.

"We can make a little salad," Laura says.

The wire really does keep the rabbits out, and most of the lettuce plants grow new leaves. Some of the seedlings get eaten by slugs, but most of the plants are managing to survive.

Every day after school, Laura and I get things ready

for our birthday celebra-
tion. First we move
the picnic table,
then we sand the
top so it doesn't have
splinters.

"Now what?" Laura
asks.

"Let's make some flower baskets," I say.

Laura has old flowerpots in her garage. We fill them
with dirt and then plant ivy in them that hangs down
the sides.

"We need a gate," I say.

Laura looks around. "We could put a log across
those two honeysuckle bushes."

"Perfect," I say, heading down the gulley to look for
a log.

It takes a while to find one the right length. Finally
Laura finds one in the tall grass near the bottom of the
hill. We drag it up together and hoist it into place.

"Our garden is really starting to look like the Secret

Garden," I say. It doesn't have climbing purple beans or chocolate cherry tomatoes or ivy crocuses like I planned. But it looks beautiful—and now Laura and I were going to have a party in it.

Laura smiles. "I never even thought we could make a garden at all."

I am trying to braid some of the ivy into a garland.

Then I see something moving behind a bush. "Hey, look," I whisper, pulling Laura toward me.

"It's him," she whispers. "I'm sure."

"White tail."

"Long whiskers."

Goo looks at us with his dark eyes and twitches his nose.

"A birthday visit," Laura whispers.

"We are the luckiest girls in the world," I say as we watch Goo hop over a branch and run into the woods.

✳ ✳ ✳